Heather's Bracelet

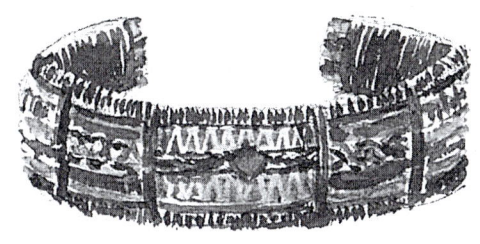

Wells Bookworms

Published by Wells Bookworms Publications, Somerset
siobhan@wellsbookworms.co.uk
www.wellsbookworms.co.uk

© Wells Bookworms 2013

All rights reserved. No part of this publication may be reproduced, stored in a retrieval system, or transmitted in any form, or by any means, electronic, mechanical, photocopying, recording or otherwise, without the prior permission of
Wells Bookworms Publications.

ISBN 9780992656706

Print Production by

St Andrews Press
THE PRINTERS

www.standrewspress.co.uk

Wells Bookworms

Violet Bevan	photography and editing
Charlotte Clissold	photography, editing and part of Chapter 5
Amy Cleverley	Chapter 1, photography
Isobell Cull	illustration, editing, cover design and page layout
Orlaith Duddy	Chapter 3
Siobhan Goodwin	(adult in charge) Chapter 8, organising, delegating, helping with everything, finishing off, refreshments!
Isabella Hiscox	Chapter 6, interviewing, research and some of the translation into Italian
Tom Humphries	illustration, editing, cover design and page layout
Izzy Jarrett	interviewing, illustration, research and photography
Oliver Johns	photography, research, editing, proof reading
Izzy Maynard	interviewing, research, Chapter 2 and editing, photography
Anna Mulvey	original idea to write the story, interviewing, organising book launch, proof reading, photography, research, chapters 4 and 7 and introduction
Cathy Pearce	interviewing, editing, Chapter 5
Lucy Phillips	interviewing, research, illustration, photography and editing
Lloyd Sharp	research, illustration, photography
Silvara White	photography, illustration, organising book launch.

Thanks

A special thanks to Heather, without whom this book would never have happened. She encouraged us from the very beginning and gave us nothing but support throughout – and biscuits! She has become our good friend.

All the people who shared their stories, memories and family photographs with us.

Michael Morpurgo for his inspiration and encouragement.

Anita Pegler, Heather's cousin for her wonderful illustration for the front cover, and the title page.

Annalisa and Isabella Hiscox and Rachele Scotto for translating the Italian edition.

Wells Twinning Association for their support with the publication of the Italian edition.

Wells Festival of Literature for helping us to provide every local school with a copy of this book.

Emily Phillips for her beautiful map.

Charlotte Bevan, Emma Bradley, Max Hale, Sarah Lean, Tara Mulvey, and Sue Purkiss for proof reading and or comments / suggestions on the book.

Jo Dymond for helping us to contact Heather.

Rebecca Gryspeerdt for her advice on the illustrations.

Barbara Spencer for her writing advice.

Philip Welch and the Wells Journal for lending research materials.

Wells and Mendip Museum for their help with the book launch (Janet, for lending us her book for research).

Tim Wood at St Andrew's Press for all his advice, patience and willingness to show the bookworms how books get from computer screen to finished product.

Henry Buckton for his generous offer to use some of his photographs.

For Heather Redman, Giuseppe and Sybil Ambrosini, Elvira Raso, Elvira Porfirio and all the people who kindly let us tell the stories of their relations.

Introduction

'Heather's Bracelet' is the work
of fifteen children aged between eight
and fifteen years, with some help from an
adult. It is set in Somerset during the Second
World War. This book is made up of two separate
stories that have been woven together. The stories
are true but some aspects of them have been
changed for the sake of the book. Some of the
photos have been taken by the children in
modern days with special effects, but some
are originals from the people whose
stories are in the book.

Places in the Story

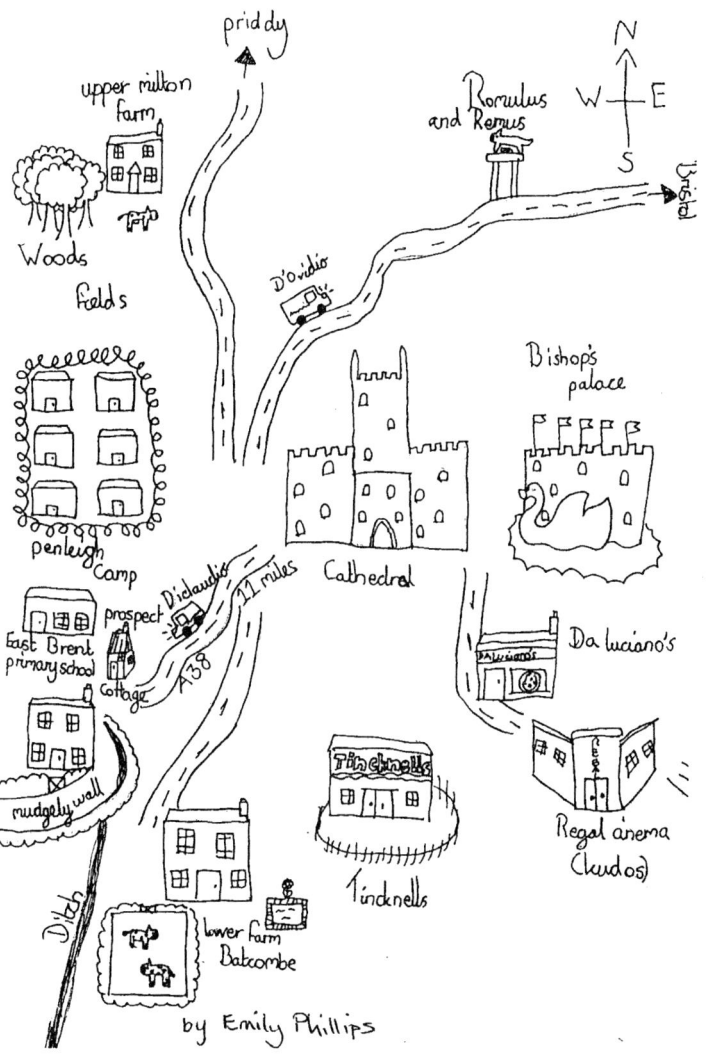

Contents

Chapter 1	Heather's Story *The Somerset Levels, May 1943*	1
Chapter 2	Heather's Story *25th May 1943, her birthday*	7
Chapter 3	German Prisoner of War's Story *The Somerset Levels, July 1943*	15
Chapter 4	Heather's Story *The Somerset Levels, July 1943*	21
Chapter 5	Giuseppe's Story *Wells, May-Sept 1943*	27
Chapter 6	Sybil's Story *Upper Milton Farm, Wells Sept 1943*	35
Chapter 7	Heather's Story *The Somerset Levels, Sept 1943*	39
Chapter 8	Seventy Years Later *Wells 2013*	47
Glossary		58
Bibliography		60

The story is set in 1943, during The Second War World

Heather
is a little girl living on the Somerset Levels.

The German Officer
is a prisoner of war in Somerset.

Giuseppe
is an Italian prisoner of war who is living and working at Penleigh Camp, Wells, Somerset.

Sybil
is a local young woman living and working on a farm near to Penleigh Camp, Wells.

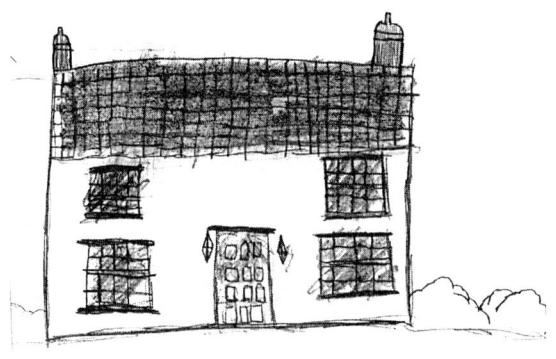

Chapter 1
Heather's Story
The Somerset Levels, May 1943

Mum said it was all because of the war that we had to move into our new house at Mudgley Wall. She said she didn't feel safe in Prospect Cottage because she thought it would get bombed. Mum had put her favourite photograph of me, and my older brother Johnny when we were little, up on the mantelpiece so it would feel like home. We didn't look like that anymore. All my lovely blonde curls had been cut off, and Johnny, now nearly eight years old, was the tallest in his class.

The photo on the mantlepiece

When dad came back from the war it was easier for my mum to cope. His chest might have been too weak to fight the Germans but it was not too weak to help at the dairy down at the farm.

I loved Prospect Cottage but at least the move meant I was living nearer my school friend Amy. I remember the first time I went to call for her, she didn't turn out to be the playmate I had hoped for. Her place was only down the lane, next to the rhyne, or ditch as some people call it. I knocked on the door but when there was no answer I knocked a second time. The door flew open and a tall, crooked lady answered.

'Who are you and what do you want?' she snapped.

The words came stammering out, 'Umm, can Amy, umm come and play umm, please?'

'She's working, doing her jobs. You can say hello but don't stay long. She is down in the yard past where the land girls are working in the barn.' I felt so awkward I ran off as fast as I could to the cobbley

Prospect Cottage

yard. Amy looked pleased to see me.

'Amy' I called, 'I can't stay long. Your Aunt said you were busy.'

'I'm glad you're here,' she huffed 'I'm worn out already.'

'I wish I was old enough to do something useful like you, Johnny and Richard. They're allowed to help at the dairy you know,' I said.

My friend Amy

'Richard? Is he the evacuee?' she asked.

'Yes, but he's not staying with us. The last ones we had were lovely but do you remember the first lot? They were horrible.' I lifted the edge of my skirt to show Amy my poor knees.

'Mum said they had *petigo* or something and that's what made my knees sore and now I have these scars.' I always tried to keep my knees covered if I could.

4

Years later I learnt that the scars were from an infectious skin disease called *impetigo*.

'You poor thing,' said Amy.

As I turned around I saw Amy's Aunt looking out of the window.

'I'd better be off,' I said and skipped away.

I had no one to play with and nothing to do, but as I set off home I suddenly remembered my birthday was only a few days away. I wondered if I might get some little treat. Mum and Dad did their best but the rations never seemed to be quite enough. I knew I probably wouldn't get a birthday cake, at least not like I'd seen in the storybooks anyway.

The first thing I heard when I walked into the kitchen back at Mudgley Wall was Mum telling Dad and Johnny that she had been right to move house. A neighbour had just told her that Prospect Cottage had been bombed the night before.

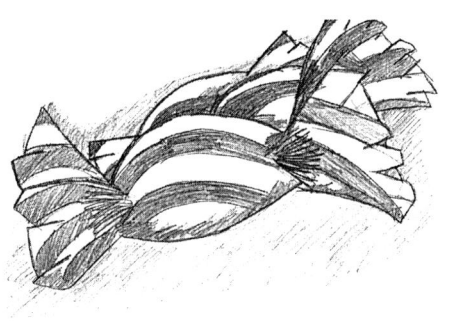

Chapter 2
Heather's Story
25th May 1943, her birthday

It was the 25th May, my birthday. I had just turned six and was so excited because Mum had promised me a trip to the cinema in Wells with Johnny. We were going to see a Roy Rogers film, 'My Pal Trigger'. I left home wearing my favourite frock.

As I got to the end of the road I turned to see my Mum waving at me. I waved back, and as Johnny walked and I skipped, there was silence apart from the occasional car passing. Suddenly a US army truck

View from the bus

appeared and as usual we shouted 'Got any gum chum?' and they threw us some sweets or 'candy' as they called it. I decided to keep mine for the film but Johnny ate his straight away.

The bus soon arrived, I remember it cost sixpence return each. It seemed like we had been travelling for ages, staring out of the window at the flat countryside to our right and The Mendip Hills to our left, when the bus stopped on the outskirts of Wells.

An old lady got on but meanwhile something had caught my eye. Out of the window I noticed a group of men in burgundy uniforms having their picture taken. I had never seen uniforms like that before, they had a big circular patch on the leg at the front and another on the back. I remember they even had a funny little dog with them. There was another man in a different uniform and he was carrying a gun.

I was able to watch for quite a while because the old lady had dropped her bag of empty lemonade bottles and the conductor was helping her to pick them up as they rolled under the seats. Eventually she came to sit beside us and she must have seen me staring out the window and pointing as I asked Johnny who the men could be.

'Don't point little girl, they're prisoners of war,' she snapped.

The man sitting to the left of the little dog must have seen me looking because at that moment he waved right at me and gave me a huge smile. I waved back. The old lady saw this and her voice softened as she said to me,

'My son is a prisoner of war in Italy. I'm sorry I snapped at you but I miss him so much.'

The Regal

Johnny asked her what prisoner of war meant and she replied,

'Well, a prisoner of war is someone that has been captured by the enemy, they must be kept safe and healthy but they have to work hard. Some people call them POW for short. They are a long way from home and don't know when they can return.' She looked sad as she spoke.

The bus pulled into the depot and so the conversation ended there. At the time I didn't really understand, and nor did Johnny, but years later I learnt about The Geneva Convention, an agreement between some countries about how prisoners of war should be kept.

We walked to 'The Regal' cinema and my brother gave the money to the lady at the desk, who looked

Waiting for the swans

very miserable. The film was fantastic and best of all I had my sweets from the US troops!

When we came out of the cinema we walked up the High St and I got to buy a jam tart from the bakers. This was a very special treat as I was the birthday girl! It tasted delicious. Having a treat like that was very rare.

I let Johnny have a bite and then he said we could go to see the swans at the Bishop's Palace because a friend had told him they rang a bell for food. When

The swans arrive

we got there I went over to a little girl who was sitting down waiting for the swans too.

'Do you know what time the swans ring the bell?' I asked.

'No, sorry,' she replied and we sat and chatted for a while as we waited. She told me her name was Violet and I remember thinking it was a pretty name. We decided to copy the other girls playing nearby and make up a clapping game. I was having such fun. Just as Johnny called over that it was time to go, the swans sailed round the corner. We followed them to the window on the gatehouse and sure enough they rang a bell and food was thrown to them from a tiny window by the gatekeeper.

What a perfect day it had been. On the bus journey home I thought about the prisoner of war who had waved at me. I wondered what it must be like for him so far away from his own country.

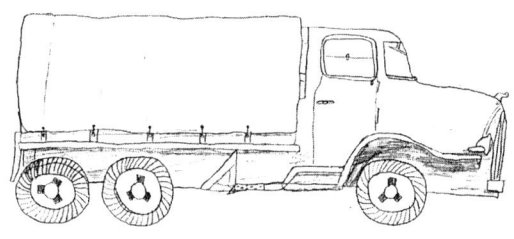

Chapter 3
German Prisoner of War's Story
The Somerset Levels, July 1943

The sun was beaming down on that hot summer's day, as I drove the truck to the Somerset Levels. Even with the canvas rolled up, I could hear all the Italian prisoners of war complaining of the heat and gasping for air.

I was a prisoner of war from Germany, an officer in the Luftwaffe, captured when I had been forced to parachute from my

The ditch at Mudgley Wall

aircraft as I was being shot down. As a senior officer I had been separated from my men as the British thought I might try to organise an escape. My job was to drive some of the Italian prisoners of war from Penleigh Camp in Wells to the Somerset Levels so that they could clear ditches.

As we arrived, I saw the ditches that the men were going to have to clear, surrounded by flat land as far as the eye could see. I could tell that this was going to be a very difficult job for them, and take a very long time and I almost in a way, felt sorry for them.

As they jumped out of the truck, their feet pounding along the ground, I set to work. You see, as I didn't have anything to do during the hours and hours that these men were working, I had found a hidden talent of mine! I discovered that I had a knack for making bracelets.

However, these weren't the ordinary bracelets that you'd find in any shop, they were completely handmade, crafted by my fingers, each one unique to itself. A spectrum of colours, woven in and out of one another, to form the structure of a semi-circle. Although they were only made of bits of old cocoa tins and coloured string I was quite proud of how they turned out. I made some money from them as they sold for two shillings and sixpence.

As I was finishing up a bracelet that I had been working on since the day before, I spotted a little girl skipping along one of the lanes towards us. She was a very pretty little girl of about six years old, sporting a sweet gingham dress. She had quite short, blonde hair and petite features. She waved at me and tried to speak, but of course I couldn't understand much of what she was saying. I did, however get the feeling that all she wanted was a friend, and so I said to myself that if she came again I would make a special bracelet just for her but keep it as a surprise.

She sat up on the wheel arch of the truck and watched me as I worked. We tried to talk but it was very difficult as we spoke different languages, however I decided to just be friendly and this seemed to make her happy. Suddenly, I heard a thump and as I turned around I saw that one of the Italian prisoners had fallen awkwardly down the side of the ditch he had been working on. I jumped out of the truck and tried to tell the little girl to go home, but as she couldn't understand what I was saying I just ushered her in the direction that she came from.

Three other men and I lifted him out of the ditch and into the truck. He was crying out in pain. The British guard told him not to worry, that Giuseppe, the new male nurse at Penleigh Camp, would have him fixed up in no time. As we drove away I saw the little girl waving, with her sweet little face and ribbon in her hair, I wondered if I would ever return to Germany and if I would ever have a family of my own and a little girl in a gingham dress.

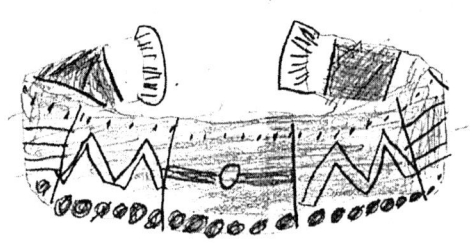

Chapter 4
Heather's Story
The Somerset Levels, July 1943

I dashed off the school bus and ran home.

'Just going up the lane, Mum', I shouted.

We had just broken up for the summer holidays and I was so excited. No more school for six weeks!

'Be back for tea,' called Mum. She didn't even look up. It was washday and mum was very busy.

I was hoping the prisoners of war would be there because I had made friends with the German officer

The school near Brent Knoll

who drove the truck. I had been down most days after school since they arrived two weeks ago. He would sit in the cab making pretty bracelets to sell from old cocoa tins and plastic string. The others, who my Mum told me were Italian, were very busy clearing out the rhynes by our house.

I spotted the truck parked in its usual place on the corner and hopped up on to the wheel arch where I always liked to sit and watch him. He greeted me with a warm smile and then, because his English still wasn't very good, he just said one word. One word I'll never forget,

'Present.'

I wondered what he meant at first. Did I need to give him a present? Then he started delving deep into his jacket pocket. His hand emerged, clutching something and he reached over and planted it in my hand. I looked down and there was a scarlet red bracelet, with sapphire blue and golden yellow. I stared at it. Then I realised he was giving it to me as a present, my eyes became blurry with tears. I looked up into his eyes that glowed bright blue. I stuttered my thank yous but then didn't know what to do or say. I wanted to throw my arms around him but I was too shy, so I quickly put the bracelet on and ran home.

I burst through the front door and the first person I saw was my Dad who looked like he'd just got in from work. He still had his overalls on.

'Look Dad, look what my officer has given me.'

'What officer's this then?' he asked

'You know, he's one of the prisoners of war working on the rhynes up the lane, except he doesn't do any digging, he drives the truck,' I replied eager to show him my bracelet.

I held out my wrist proudly but as I saw the look on his face and the frown appearing on his brow I

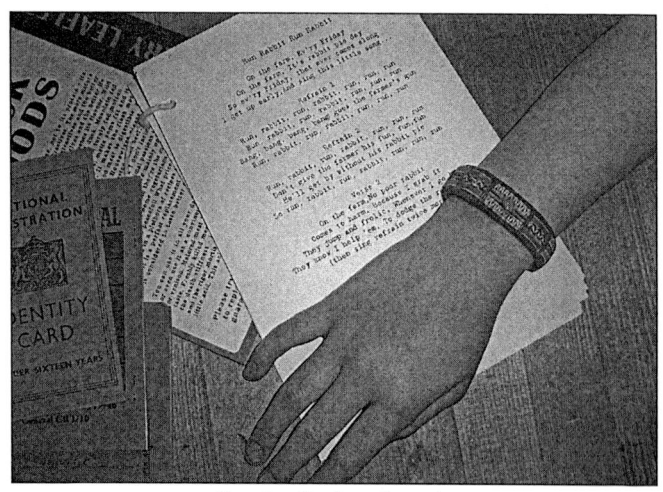
Showing Dad my bracelet

realised I had made a big mistake.

'Are you telling me that I risked my life fighting those Germans only for my own daughter to go round making friends with one of them?' he shouted.

I had never seen Dad so angry. I was too scared to say anything back.

Mum came in wanting to know what all the shouting was about. We each tried to put our side of the story but when Mum realised what was going on she stood up straight, looked my Dad in the eye and said,

'He is someone's son. I don't expect they want the war any more than we do. Now we'll say no more about it.'

I took a quick glance over at my Dad. I could tell by his fiery eyes that he was still angry but he didn't dare say anything else.

I crept upstairs and hid my bracelet under my pillow. Fancy a German officer making me a special bracelet. From what a lot of people had been saying about the Germans I had thought they would be horrible but my officer was so very kind and really he seemed just like one of us, except that he couldn't speak much English. I wondered what he thought of us, and of being so far away from his family and friends. I remembered the man who had waved at me on my birthday and the old lady's son over in Italy. Sometimes the war didn't seem to make much sense to me.

I heard Johnny calling me down to tea. I knew it would just be bread and butter and a plain biscuit or two but I could never stomach much of the school dinners and so I was really hungry. I went down the stairs and sat at the table. I tried not to catch Dad's eye.

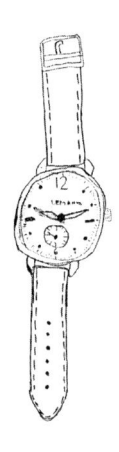

Chapter 5
Giuseppe's Story
Wells, May-Sept 1943

I will always remember the very first day that I met Sybil. I had been a prisoner of war at Penleigh Camp on the outskirts of Wells for only a couple of weeks. I was a nurse, like I had been in the Italian Army, and it was my job to assist the doctor in the camp. I had settled in easily and we were treated very well.

It was a sunny day in May and I had just come

out of the medical building. It was so hot that all I really wanted to do was to have a cool drink and a rest but my friends were waiting outside for me.

'Hey, Giuseppe! Come for a walk with us!' shouted Angelo.

'No thanks' I replied, but they wouldn't take no for an answer. I often look back now and feel so grateful that they persisted. A large group of us ended up walking out of the camp accompanied by our guard and his little dog. There were woods ahead and we were pleased to get in some shade for a while.

We chatted along the way and I remember my friend Angelo talking about his work at Lower Farm, Batcombe and the dog there called Monty who reminded him of his dog back in Italy. His friend Gaetano, who had also worked there, told us about the beautiful fishponds he had built for the farmer. We were all so far from home and missing our families but we tried to make the best of it.

Upper Milton Farm

Many of the men at the camp worked on local farms like my friend Manfredi. He said that the family he worked for were very good to him and I remember he told us that once they lent him a bicycle so he could go to Weston-Super-Mare. The bike had been stolen on the High St when he had nipped into a shop, but luckily he had managed to get a lift back to the camp. The very next day a police officer had shown up at the farm. At first Manfredi had been worried but it turned out that the officer was only bringing him the bike back! We had a good laugh about that.

Some men worked in Wells and one man, also called Giuseppe, worked at a firm called Tincknells. He was just telling us how much he enjoyed the work there and what a good boss he had, when we began walking up a very steep hill towards a large farm. I had no idea how my life would change within the next few minutes.

Our guard knocked at the door of the farmhouse. A lady answered and he asked if we could all get a drink of water. She agreed and we followed her across the yard.

'Just go in there, the tap's on the left just past where my daughter is working,' she said and then called out 'Sybil these men are just coming in for a drink.'

We went in and my heart started beating a little faster because sitting at the table was a beautiful young woman, who I now knew was called Sybil. Her hair was dark brown and she wore a pink, flowery dress. She sat on a stool churning butter, concentrating hard. She had a kind face and she looked like someone you could trust. I turned around and murmured to my friend,

'One day she will be my wife.'

She glanced up and I felt my insides melt. It was such a wonderful moment. I made a vow to myself that I would return and that I would talk to her one day and get to know her. I was desperate to see her again. As we returned to the camp my mind was filled with thoughts of the beautiful young woman.

Just as we came to the main road our guard produced a camera and said we were all to have a group photograph. He was always good to us and we had a great deal of respect for him. As we posed for the camera the little dog jumped into my friend's arms as we knelt down at the centre of the group. I looked towards the camera and noticed a bus pull up and a sweet little girl was pointing and peering out of the window. I gave her a big wave and she waved back. I was still smiling as the camera clicked. I can still remember her face now, so innocent. Of course she had no idea why I was so happy! I have kept that photo ever since.

Giuseppe's Photo

Unlike some of the other POWs at Penleigh Camp, I was allowed out by myself at certain times. This was because I was a nurse and had not been trained in combat. I still had to wear my special burgundy uniform with identifying patches on the front and back so that everyone would know I was a POW. This meant that only a few days later I could return to Upper Milton Farm by myself. I had spent a long time practising the English words in my head. I had checked them carefully in the English / Italian dictionary in the doctor's office.

I can still remember it as if it was yesterday, walking along by a high wall and then finding Sybil out in the yard, having just milked the cows. We smiled at each other. I tried talking to her but my mouth opened and closed like a goldfish and it felt dry like sand so I gave up and decided to talk to her next time. It was the following day that I finally plucked up the courage to speak.

'Miss, what time is it?' I asked nervously.

I don't think I should have said that because as she was about to answer me she looked at my wrist. I was wearing my watch! She laughed, flicking the hair out of her face and went back to her work smiling. Even though I was a bit embarrassed I felt great – I had finally spoken to her. I was grinning from ear to ear with happiness as I set off back to the camp.

Over the next few months I kept on going back to see her, loving every second, even giving her romantic notes. I began wrapping her mother around my little finger. I had been a builder back in Italy and so in my spare time I repaired walls and replaced the kitchen floor. I must have made a good impression. They always treated me as one of the family.

It was in September that we got the news that Italy had been liberated. We were now on the same side as the British but that didn't mean we could go home yet. Still, I was so happy about the news that I began to think about my future. That day I went to see Sybil again, my beauty. I slid a note into her delicate hand. It read ' Much war finish make matrimony'. From the first moment I had seen her I had wanted her to be my wife and now she knew too.

Sybil

Chapter 6

Sybil's Story

Upper Milton Farm, Wells Sept 1943

It had been four months since Giuseppe had first come to Upper Milton Farm, when he had seen me in the dairy. It was a few days later that he had come back and asked me the time, when he was wearing his watch all along! He continued coming almost every day, just when he knew I would be fetching the cows in for milking. After a while he started giving me romantic notes, notes that I kept in a very special silver painted drawer in my room and one by one I would look at them every day.

At first I had thought that my family might not approve of me courting a POW but they had welcomed him and had all grown very fond of him, especially my mother who he charmed by doing skilful buildings jobs in the house.

Giuseppe at Upper Milton Farm

I would be in the dairy hand milking the cows, peering out until I saw his figure striding through the long green grass as it swayed in the wind. He would walk towards the farmhouse, and as I saw his handsome face my heart would begin thumping. I would rush out and he would say 'Bellissima, my beauty.'

The woods near the farm

Sometimes if we had time we would go for a walk in the woods and he would slip his hand into mine. We would trample through the sticks and leaves perfectly content. Once I remember looking up as I heard two birds tweeting, I saw them put their heads together and I realised they were in love. Later when we returned to the farmhouse, Giuseppe would slip a note into my hand and kiss my cheek. As I watched him wander back to Penleigh Camp I would carefully open the note.

I will always remember that day in September

1943 that he came, so happy to hear about the liberation of Italy. He spoke of his family and friends at home and said that even though he had been getting letters he wanted to see them, talk to them. We both knew that him going back to Italy was a long way off. It was that day that he gave me the note that said ' Much war finish, make matrimony.'

I read it again and again, completely stunned. He wanted to marry me once the war had finished. I dashed into the kitchen to show my mother. She just smiled and we both joked that he probably wasn't serious. Although I pretended not to take it too seriously, secretly I wished it could happen.

Chapter 7
Heather's Story
The Somerset Levels, Sept 1943

I ran home from school, a glimmer of happiness chiming through my body, and then it seemed to fall out. I looked over at the rhyne but there was no truck there. Where was my officer? Would he remember me? I went right to the corner where he usually parked and that's when it struck me. The rhyne was finally cleared, their work was finished. I was so sad. I ran back home, my

The cleared rhyne

eyes filled with tears.

'Mum! My officer's gone. What shall I do? Where's he gone? Will he come back?' I spluttered.

'Oh Heather. They've just moved onto a different place. You probably won't see him again but at least you have that pretty bracelet as a reminder of him.'

'Yes, but Mum I really want to see him again. He was so kind to me. I just want to say goodbye properly,' I cried.

'You will have to get on with it my girl. There are plenty of people suffering worse than just losing a friend. There is a war on. Come on, pull yourself together.'

I kept muttering on for a while but Mum was only half listening because she was busy making an apple pie.

'Oooh that pie looks delicious. What a treat!' I said. The sight of the pie cheered me up and my mouth started watering.

'I must make a good job of it. We are to send a slice over to Mr Johns next door. He saw Johnny and Richard looking longingly at his apple tree and he said they could help themselves as long as he got some of the pie. The boys hadn't realised they were cooking apples!'

I was looking forward to eating it but I was still feeling sad about losing my officer. I went to my room for a private cry. Then I heard the familiar bang click click of our front door and I heard the deep smiling voice of my Dad's friend from Wells, Uncle Ted.

'Heather, Johnny,' he called.

I ran down the stairs and hugged him tightly.

'Here you are my lovely,' he said as he handed me one of his precious butterscotch sweets that he always brought just for us.

'Thanks Uncle Ted. You always manage to pick just the right moment to visit.'

'Well I can't stay long tonight because I am on my way to a Home Guard meeting in the Bishop's Barn in Wells. You know I'm too old to fight but I still want to do my bit.'

He walked through to the front room to talk to Dad and I followed him and got up onto his knee. I didn't understand a lot of what they were talking about but I do remember them mentioning Percy Jarrett, one of our neighbours, who was a fireman in the RAF and was home on leave. One of Uncle Ted's relations, Dickie Bird, who was a driver in the army, was also spoken about. I remember that because

Dad said his real name was Albert but everyone called him Dickie and they both laughed about it. I didn't understand why that was so funny at the time.

They chatted on for a while and I remember wondering why they kept talking about Italy so much. My ears pricked up when I heard them talking about the British prisoners of war over there. Before long though, Uncle Ted got up and I hopped down from his lap. He headed off to catch the next bus into Wells as I waved goodbye from the door.

Richard, Johnny's friend who was the evacuee, stayed to tea and I remember him saying how lucky we were to live in the countryside where it was safer. He said we had much better food too than in the big towns and cities. As I saw Mum pouring the custard on the warm apple pie I did feel lucky that father worked at the dairy. I felt lucky too that I was with my parents and that I hadn't been evacuated like him and so many others. I tasted every mouthful of that pie. I was just daydreaming about my officer and my lovely bracelet when Mum began shooing us from the table. Johnny had to take our neighbour Mr Johns his piece of pie. I couldn't get used to thinking of him as Captain Johns now he was in the army, Dad said he was only home on leave with his parents for a few days before he had to go back fighting again.

Later that evening I had to help Mum and Dad sort out the blackout. We put the black material at the windows to block out every chink of light just in case a bomber saw it and dropped a bomb on our house. My thoughts whizzed round my head about what could happen to us. Would we be safe? After all Prospect Cottage had been bombed a few months ago. I pushed these thoughts out of my mind and scampered upstairs to get ready for bed.

The first thing I did was check my bracelet was safe under my pillow. I got ready for bed and said goodnight to Mum and Dad. I hadn't told anyone but I was scared of the dark and I hated the blackout. I lay there thinking about all the awful things that were happening because of the war, people we knew and loved fighting our enemies, getting hurt or even dying. I was so confused, after all hadn't I made

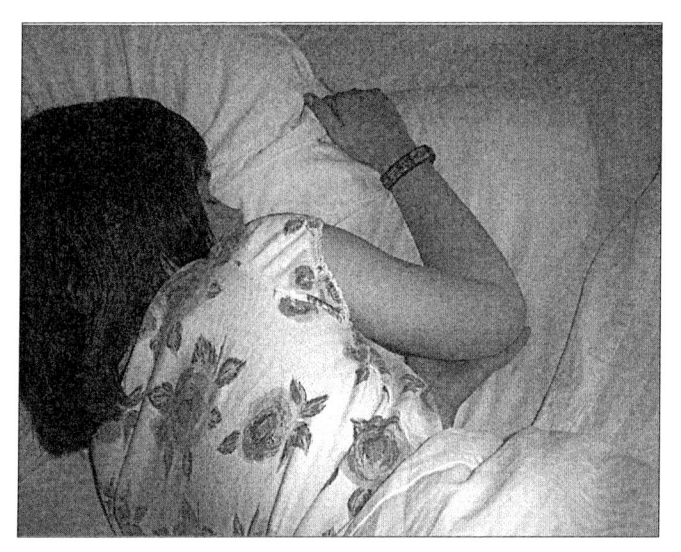

Dreaming of life after the war

friends with one of our enemies? I suppose in one way my officer was our enemy really but to me he had been a kind friend and I promised myself that I would never forget him. I felt under my pillow again and there it was, my bracelet. I slipped it on my wrist. I must have fallen asleep because I had dreams about my officer coming back to The Somerset Levels after the war was over, good dreams that I wished would come true.

Chapter 8
Seventy Years Later
Wells 2013

In 2012 a group of children called Wells Bookworms, began reading a book called 'Little Manfred' by Michael Morpurgo. It was all about the friendships formed during the Second World War by two POWs working on a farm in England, and in particular a toy that they made for a little girl. The children enjoyed the book and asked lots of questions about POWs.

The lady who ran Wells Bookworms was very interested in the war and when she heard there was an exhibition on in Wells and Mendip Museum she decided to go and visit. When she got there she saw a display of writing about local people's memories of the war, lots of old photographs and many items of interest.

As she was peering into a glass display cabinet she spotted a small colourful bracelet. Beside it was written 'This bracelet was made for a little girl by a German prisoner of war'. Straight away she thought of 'Little Manfred' and couldn't wait to tell the bookworms what she had found. She wished she could contact the owner of the bracelet and that is what happened.

You have probably guessed by now that Heather was the owner of the bracelet and I was the lady who went to the museum. Heather came to visit the bookworms and she told them all about the kind man who had made the bracelet for her seventy years ago, and how she had always treasured it since. One of the bookworms said that they should write Heather's story just like Michael Morpurgo had written about 'Little Manfred'. A few weeks later the bookworms got to meet Michael Morpurgo and they told him how his book had inspired them. He encouraged them to keep reading and writing and that's what they did.

They began researching the book, visiting the places where Heather lived, learning about life on the Home Front. The bookworms met lots of other people living in and around Wells and asked them about their wartime memories too. Two of the people they met were Giuseppe and Sybil Ambrosini. The bookworms really wanted to include such a romantic story. The other characters in the story are people who the bookworms are related to, who they have got to know through friends at school, or who are made up (Violet and the old lady on the bus).

Many of the prisoners of war had good experiences during their time in the Wells area and this was what the bookworms focussed on. It is important to record though that a few did experience some prejudice and hostility even long after the war was over.

The mother of Bookworm Isabella Hiscox, who is Italian, offered to translate the book into Italian with the help of her daughter and niece, so that Italian people near and far could read the story in their native language.

The bookworms, all aged between eight and fifteen years old, worked hard to take photographs, interview people, draw illustrations, write chapters, edit chapters, proof read chapters, design the cover, choose the fonts and page layout, apply for an ISBN number, write to local organisations asking for their support and organise a book launch.

If you would like to visit some of the places mentioned in the story, then have a look at the map. The rhyne is at Mudgley Wall, Rooksbridge off the A38. The Romulus and Remus statue is by the A39 near Penn Hill outside Wells (this is a very busy road). Penleigh Camp was on Wookey Hole Road in Wells but in 2013 you will only see more modern buildings on the site behind the metal fence.

So that is how this book came about. Perhaps if you come across an interesting story one day you might be inspired to do what the bookworms did and write it down so others can enjoy it too. Remember, you never know what might happen once you pick up a book, or if you decide to visit a museum one day.

To make an interesting story with lots of people's lives in, we had to change some parts a little bit. Below are the true facts of who people were and what happened to them after the war.

Heather still lives and works locally and she still treasures her bracelet. She never knew the name of the German officer and she never saw him again but she has not forgotten him. She married John Redman and they had four children, Rachel, John, Robert and Steven and four grandchildren, Charlotte, Sam, Daniel and Alexander.

Heather's brother Johnny worked at The Mendip Hospital for many years. Heather's Mum and Dad lived on The Levels for the rest of their lives. After the war one of the evacuees who came to live with Heather's family stayed on to work at a local farm where he remained for the rest of his life.

Giuseppe Ambrosini and ***Sybil*** married after the war. Giuseppe, along with many other Italian POWs was repatriated in 1946. Not long after they returned to England and settled in Wells. They set up their own building firm and over the years many Italian people came to work for them. Giuseppe still calls Sybil 'my beauty' and he really was wearing a watch when he asked her the time! They live less than a mile from where they first met.

They had two children, Raymond and Luana, five grandchildren, Mark, Adrian, Tanya, Joanna and Martin and fifteen great grandchildren, Emily, Olivia, Aimee, Melessa, Naomi, Sophie, Max, Hollie, Pepe, Luca, Toto, Maggie, Aldo, Thea and Milo.

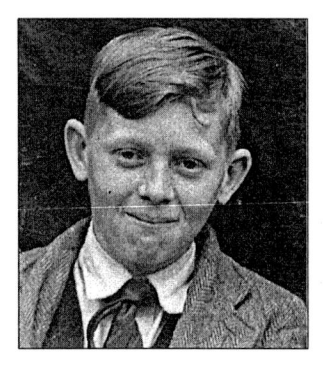

Richard (Johnny's friend in the story) is Bookworm Lloyd Sharp's grandad. He was an evacuee but not here in Somerset.

Captain Norman Johns (Heather's neighbour in the story) fought in the D-Day landings. He was the grandfather of Bookworm Oliver Johns.

Ted Goodwin *(Uncle Ted in the story) was a member of the Home Guard but in Lincolnshire, not in Somerset. He was Bookworm Anna Mulvey's great grandad and Bookworm Leader Siobhan Goodwin's Grandad (and he loved butterscotch).*

Percy Jarrett *was a fireman in the RAF. He was Bookworm Izzy Jarrett's great grandfather.*

Angelo Cristofoli *was a POW at Penleigh. His nephew, Bruno who travelled from Italy and came to work at Lower Farm after the war, was a good friend of Bookworm Isabella Hiscox's Italian grandfather.*

Giuseppe Porfirio *was a POW at Penleigh Camp. He worked at Tincknells in Wells during the war and then was asked to return from Italy after the war by Tincknells where he worked all of his life. He married Elvira and they had three children, Anna Teresa, Francesco and Clara and five grandchildren, Hannah, Sophia, Thomas, Lisa and Stefania.*

Giuseppe arranged for his good friend Antonio Diclaudio to get work locally after the war. Antonio travelled from Italy with his wife Rosa (née D'Ovidio) and they had three children, Umberto, Mariano, and Natalino and nine grandchildren, Anthony, Trisha, Nicola, Simon, Mitchell, Levi, Sapphire, Loren and Kirsty. You will recognise the name D'Ovidio from the building firm, and the name Diclaudio from the plumbing firm, both based locally.

***Gaetano Celestra** was a POW at Penleigh Camp. In his spare time, after he had done his work on Beechbarrow Farm near Wells he built the Romulus and Remus statue that still stands today by the A39. He built it to show his appreciation for all the kindness that he and his friends had been shown by local people. He told Angelo Cristofoli that he had modelled the wolf from the statue on Monty the farm*

Gaetano's fish pond, Lower Farm, Batcombe

If there hadn't been Italian prisoners here I would never be here. The Italian prisoner of war (Angelo Cristofoli) who replaced Gaetano at Lower Farm brought his nephew (Bruno) over to England because there weren't many jobs in Italy. Then Bruno married Gill (the farmer's daughter). My Italian grandfather was friends with Bruno's family in Italy and that's why my Mum visited England and met my Dad. *(by Bookworm Isabella Hiscox) dog. Gill, (the farmer's daughter who married Bruno, Angelo Cristofoli's nephew) still has childhood memories of Gaetano coming back to Lower Farm, Batcombe to measure Monty, and how difficult it was to keep the dog still! Gaetano had worked at Lower Farm and built two fishponds there, before he went up to Beechbarrow Farm.*

Manfredi Raso was a POW but not in Wells, he was in Goathurst Camp near Bridgwater. After the war he worked on a farm at Rodney Stoke for the same family he had worked for during the war. He met Elvira and they married and had three children, Lina, Roberto and Claudio. His brother, Michele and his wife Celestina came over to Wells and had three children, Silvio, Luciano, and Franca and six grandchildren, Alessandro, Maranella, Oriana, Santino, Marcello and Giovanni. You will recognise one of the names in the restaurant on Broad St in Wells – Da Luciano.

Luciano's wife, Angelina Raso (née Ferrari) has helped the bookworms to gather this information. Her brother, Frank Ferrari, runs Bar Italia on Broad Street too.

Dickie Bird *was a driver in the army. He fought in the D-Day landings. He rode a motorcycle behind enemy lines through parts of Germany. At times it was so dangerous that he had to drive with his head and chest on top of the petrol tank to avoid being injured on wires put across the roads. He was Bookworm Lloyd Sharp's great grandad.*

Glossary

Bellissima	Italian for 'my beauty'
Blackout	*during the war light had to be blocked from the windows so the enemy couldn't see a target for their bombs. This was usually done with a heavy black material.*
Courting	*an old fashioned word for 'going out' with someone.*
Evacuee	*a child from a busy city moved to the country to avoid bombing*
Geneva Convention	*an agreement between countries to look after POWs properly*
Home Front	*how people lived in Britain during WW2*
Home Guard	*men who were perhaps too old or unwell to serve in the war who would defend their country if it was invaded*
Land Girls	*members of the Women's Land Army who worked on farms during WW2*
Liberation of Italy	*when Britain and their allies freed Italy from the Germans*
Luftwaffe	*the German equivalent of the RAF*

Matrimony	*marriage*
POW	*prisoner of war, someone who is captured and kept securely by the enemy*
RAF	*the Royal Air Force*
Repatriation	*returning soldiers, including POWs to their own country after a war*
Rhyne	*a Somerset word for a drainage ditch*
Romulus and Remus	*a legend telling of twin brothers who as babies were saved by a wolf. Romulus is said to have founded Rome in Italy.*
Second World War	*the war which affected many countries throughout the world 1939-1945 (also known as WW2)*
Somerset Levels	*an area of flat land, once under water but that has been drained over the centuries.*

Bibliography

War on the Home Front *by Juliet Gardiner*

A History of Penleigh *by Fred Davis*

Seeing it Through Wells at War 1939-45 *One Hundred and Seventh Annual report of Wells Natural History and Archaeological Society 1995*